Quint and
Miss Jessel at Bly

by Don Nigro

A SAMUEL FRENCH ACTING EDITION

SAMUEL
FRENCH

FOUNDED 1830

NEW YORK HOLLYWOOD LONDON TORONTO

SAMUELFRENCH.COM

IMPORTANT BILLING AND CREDIT REQUIREMENTS

All producers of *QUINT AND MISS JESSEL AT BLY* must give credit to the Author of the Play in all programs distributed in connection with performances of the Play, and in all instances in which the title of the Play appears for the purposes of advertising, publicizing or otherwise exploiting the Play and/or a production. The name of the Author *must* appear on a separate line on which no other name appears, immediately following the title and *must* appear in size of type not less than fifty percent of the size of the title type.

QUINT AND MISS JESSEL AT BLY was first produced at Theatre X in Milwaukee, Wisconsin in March and April of 2000. The production was directed by John Kishline with the following cast:

MASTER OF BLY...................................Jonathan West
PETER QUINT ....Timothy Reynolds
MISS JESSEL .... Alix Martin

In June and July of 2001, *QUINT AND MISS JESSEL AT BLY* was produced at The People's Light And Theatre Company in Malvern, Pennsylvania. The production was directed by Peter De Laurier with the following cast:

MASTER OF BLY................................. Graham Smith
PETER QUINT ....John Luria
MISS JESSEL ....Mary Elizabeth Scallen

QUINT AND MISS JESSEL AT BLY was produced by Random Arts, Inc. at Theatre 22 in New York City in April of 2002. The production was directed by Nicole Lerario with the following cast and crew:

MASTER OF BLY.................................. Carl Bradford
PETER QUINT .... Jason Jennings
MISS JESSEL ....A. Caitlin Carr

Assistant Director – Robert Kimbro
Stage Manager – Thomas Weitz
Costumes – Staci Shember
Lighting Design – Ian W. Hill
Technical Director – Ed Sellick
Sound Design – Mike Bazini
Associate Producer – Adrienne Onofir
Wig Mistress – Danielle Masterson
Graphic Designer – Daniel Kleinfeld
Electrics – Bob Balough

CHARACTERS

THE MASTER OF BLY – A man in his thirties.
PETER QUINT – His valet, thirties.
MISS JESSEL – A woman in her twenties.

SETTING

The middle years of the nineteenth century. All locations are present simultaneously on one simple unit set which will represent at various times a residence in Harley Street, London, a bench in Regent's Park, and several locations at Bly, a country house in Essex: the library, the parlor, the tower, the lake, a small boat, the foot of the staircase, etc. Darkness and shadows predominate. The players move easily and in character from one scene to the next, often without leaving the stage. Each part of the set may represent more than one location in different scenes, as what any give part of the set represents at any given moment depends entirely upon how the characters are using it. This fluidity of movement and transition is absolutely essential. The way the play moves is always a part of the play.

No, no,—there are depths, depths! The more I go over it, the more I see in it, and the more I see in it, the more I fear. I don't know what I don't see—what I don't fear!

I had made of her a receptacle of lurid things.

– Henry James, *The Turn of the Screw*

ACT ONE

1.

(Lights up on the **MASTER OF BLY** *and* **PETER QUINT**, *his valet, sitting and drinking together one evening by the light of an invisible downstage fire at the Master's residence in Harley Street, London. The* **MASTER** *sits in his comfortable chair down right,* **QUINT** *on a love seat nearby, with a small table in between.)*

MASTER. I've been rather good to you, on the whole, over the years, have I not, Quint?

QUINT. You've been exceedingly good to me, sir. Surprisingly good. In fact, if I may take the liberty of saying so, it is nearly indecent how good you have been to me.

MASTER. I know you're not in the best of health.

QUINT. I'm not?

MASTER. No. You're not.

QUINT. No, I suppose I'm not. I suppose I'm not in the best of health, am I?

MASTER. So I'm sending you to the country.

QUINT. To the country?

MASTER. Yes.

QUINT. You're sending me to the country?

MASTER. For your health.

QUINT. For my health? You're sending me to the country for my health?

MASTER. To Bly.

QUINT. To Bly? You're sending me to Bly?

MASTER. It's not as if you haven't been there before.

7

QUINT. Yes, I've been there before. I've been there with you.

MASTER. Well, of course with me. Who else?

QUINT. So you're coming too?

MASTER. I am perhaps coming, now and then, early on, for brief periods of time, when I can get away, just to look in on you, see how things are going, and after that I have no doubt I will be popping in from time to time to say hello, change horses, come in out of the rain, as it were.

QUINT. You're sending me to the country, and you're not coming?

MASTER. That's pretty much it, yes.

QUINT. But I'm your valet.

MASTER. I know what you are, Quint.

QUINT. What will I do there?

MASTER. Oh, I shouldn't worry too much about that. You've always found ways of amusing yourself there in the past, haven't you?

QUINT. Yes, but then I was your valet. What will I be now?

MASTER. You'll be the – overseer.

QUINT. The overseer?

MASTER. Yes.

QUINT. What the hell is that?

MASTER. Well, it's a sort of a – caretaker. Yes. The Caretaker of Bly. That's what you'll be.

QUINT. I shall be damned lonely there, that's what I'll be.

MASTER. Nonsense. You'll have company. Mrs Grose will be there.

QUINT. Mrs Grose?

MASTER. Yes. Mrs Grose is very fond of you.

QUINT. Mrs Grose detests me. Mrs Grose would quite happily see me castrated and decapitated on the croquet lawn. She'd make a picnic lunch out of my liver. Mrs Grose is a great, fat, stupid, gossiping sow.

MASTER. Don't worry, Quint. You'll have her eating out of your hand in no time, I'm sure, if you put your mind to it. You're an extremely charming and resourceful fellow. That's why I'm trusting you with the children.

QUINT. What children?

MASTER. My younger brother's children.

QUINT. You're giving me your younger brother's children?

MASTER. Well, I must do something with them.

QUINT. Why?

MASTER. Because he's dead.

QUINT. He's dead? Your brother is dead?

MASTER. In India.

QUINT. Your brother is dead in India?

MASTER. In the Punjab. I think it's the Punjab. Some place hot. Is the Punjab hot, Quint? I think the Punjab is hot.

QUINT. What about your brother's wife?

MASTER. No, she's not hot. Well, I suppose she was hot at one time, but now she's dead, too.

QUINT. They're both dead?

MASTER. Yes.

QUINT. In the Punjab?

MASTER. Or thereabouts.

QUINT. Were they eaten by crocodiles?

MASTER. No, I believe it was some sort of tropical fever. Warmth is nearly always fatal to the British, I am told. In any case, they're dead, and I've inherited the children.

QUINT. And you're giving them to me?

MASTER. I'm not giving them to you. I'm putting them in your charge. I'm sending them to Bly, where you are going to take care of them. Hence your title, the Caretaker of Bly.

QUINT. I thought you were sending me there for my health.

MASTER. It is for your health. But, as long as you're going to be there anyway, I thought you might as well look after the children for me.

QUINT. But what am I going to do with children?

MASTER. Nothing much, I should think. Mrs Grose will give you a hand.

QUINT. Mrs Grose is an imbecile.

MASTER. But a good woman and an excellent housekeeper. And, frankly, Quint, I have always suspected that Mrs Grose has a little thing for you.

QUINT. Well, that's good news. I'm to be packed off to the country with two orphaned children and an imbecilic old woman who has a little thing.

MASTER. And Miss Jessel, of course.

QUINT. Miss Jessel.

MASTER. The governess. I've engaged a governess. Miss Jessel.

QUINT. You've engaged Miss Jessel.

MASTER. I have indeed. Mrs Grose is to keep the house. Miss Jessel will govern the children. And you are to be the caretaker.

QUINT. I am to take care of them all.

MASTER. Now you've got it.

QUINT. You've planned this all out rather carefully, sir, if I may say so.

MASTER. Thank you, Quint. I do my best.

QUINT. Are there going to be rabbits? Must I also take care of rabbits? Because I absolutely draw the line at rabbits. That is a line I will not cross.

MASTER. I don't know about rabbits. The question of rabbits is one which we shall perhaps take up at some later date. The children, however, arrive from India next week, so you must go down to Bly tomorrow. I'll look in when I can, to make sure things are running smoothly. And I shall expect things to run smoothly, Quint. You know I have a morbid distaste for chaos of any sort. Although I suppose there is only one sort of chaos, isn't there? At any rate, these abstruse philosophical ruminations notwithstanding, if all seems in order, I shall be able to turn my attention for the most part towards my affairs in London and leave the keys to the kingdom, as it were, more or less entirely in your hands. I have great faith in you, Quint. I know you'll rise to the occasion. You always rise to the occasion. Well, nearly always. I think you should consider it a great honor, being entrusted with my poor dead brother's children. You do consider it an honor, don't you, Quint? Quint?

QUINT. You've always been very good to me, sir.

MASTER. I have, haven't I?

QUINT. Yes, you have.

(Pause.)

MASTER. Well, that's settled then. Good man. Down the hatch, Quint.

QUINT. Yes. Down the hatch.

(They drink. Lights fade on them.)

2

(Sound of birds singing as lights come up on **MISS JESSEL** *arranging flowers in the parlor at Bly, up left.* **QUINT** *has simply risen, gone around the back of the love seat, turned to* **MISS JESSEL,** *and moved quite naturally into the light and thus into the scene with her. The* **MASTER** *remains sitting in his chair in London, visible and in character, not frozen, drinking, just out of the light.)*

QUINT. So, did you enjoy having the Master?

MISS JESSEL. I beg your pardon?

QUINT. Did you enjoy having the Master here at Bly?

MISS JESSEL. Yes, I did. Very much. Didn't you?

QUINT. Oh, yes. It was the highlight of my youth. You seem to get on well with him.

MISS JESSEL. He has been very good to me.

QUINT. Yes. Me too.

(Pause.)

So, how exactly did you come to find yourself in this position?

MISS JESSEL. What do you mean?

QUINT. I mean how exactly did you come to find yourself in this position? Here. At Bly. As the Governess at Bly. As the lady who has been entrusted with the nurturing of the minds and souls of dear little Miles and Florence.

MISS JESSEL. Flora.

QUINT. Dear little Miles and Flora. How did you, of all people, end up here, in this lovely situation? Did you answer an advertisement in the newspaper?

MISS JESSEL. No.

QUINT. Well, how then did you become aware that this position was opening up, as it were? I mean, it's difficult for one to fill a position, is it not, unless one has somehow become aware that such and such a position has in fact opened up? How do you come to be here,

Miss Jessel? After all, you are something of a lady, are you not?

MISS JESSEL. Of course I am a lady.

QUINT. Are you perhaps a friend of the family?

MISS JESSEL. I was acquainted in my girlhood with the children's mother.

QUINT. Ah. So you were an intimate friend and bosom companion of the younger brother's dead wife, were you? The poor late mother of dear little Miles and Dora?

MISS JESSEL. Flora.

QUINT. So you were previously acquainted with the Master as well, perhaps?

MISS JESSEL. Slightly.

QUINT. You were slightly acquainted with the Master of Bly, prior to your coming here?

MISS JESSEL. Only very slightly.

QUINT. Well, you must have made quite an impression on him. I mean, after such a slight acquaintance, to entrust such a slight acquaintance as yourself, albeit a lady, and a very beautiful lady, if I may say so, but, nonetheless, a young and rather inexperienced lady – you are relatively inexperienced, are you not? One can see merely by looking at you that you are young, but experience is a more difficult thing to gage – to entrust you, after only a slight acquaintance, with the infinitely precious minds and souls of two dear, dear little children like Max and Flora –

MISS JESSEL. Miles.

QUINT. Max and Miles.

MISS JESSEL. Miles and Flora.

QUINT. You must have made a very great impression indeed upon the Master of Bly, who is, as is well known, a person of exquisite taste. And he, no doubt, made quite an impression upon you, as well. Did the Master of Bly not make a great impression upon you, Miss Jessel?

MISS JESSEL. He is a rather impressive gentleman.

QUINT. He is, isn't he? And were you as well slightly acquainted with me, before coming here, before your advent at Bly?

MISS JESSEL. With you?

QUINT. Yes. Were you previously acquainted with me?

MISS JESSEL. Don't you know?

QUINT. I suppose I should know, shouldn't I? And I rather think I would remember having met a personage so lovely as you. But you see, I have not been well. I have not been well at all. I was sent down here, to Bly, for my health, you know. And one of the more distressing symptoms of my unfortunate state of ill health, you see, Miss Jessel, is that my memory is –

(Pause.)

MISS JESSEL. Is what?

QUINT. What?

MISS JESSEL. Your memory is what?

QUINT. My memory is what?

MISS JESSEL. You were speaking of your memory.

QUINT. Was I? What was I saying about it?

MISS JESSEL. I don't know. I presume that it was defective.

QUINT. Is it? Is my memory defective?

MISS JESSEL. That was my presumption.

QUINT. That was your presumption, was it?

MISS JESSEL. Yes. It was.

QUINT. And how do you like Bly, Miss Jessel?

MISS JESSEL. I like it fine, Mr Quint.

QUINT. You don't have bad dreams?

MISS JESSEL. Bad dreams?

QUINT. Because the truth is, Miss Jessel, if I may take the liberty of referring to you as Miss Jessel, the truth is, if one may be permitted to speak of the truth here, in this place, at this time, at least among ourselves, at any rate, when the long day's work is done, with our feet up on the kettle and cigars in our mouths, as it were, the truth is that ever since I came down here, to Bly, I've been having bad dreams.

MISS JESSEL. How distressing for you.

QUINT. More distressing than you can possibly imagine, Miss Jessel. The fact is, you're in them.

MISS JESSEL. I am in your dreams?

QUINT. You're the chief attraction. I won't bore you with the details.

MISS JESSEL. Thank you, Mr Quint.

QUINT. I wouldn't bring it up at all, were it not for the fact that the children are also having bad dreams.

MISS JESSEL. No they're not.

QUINT. Yes they are.

MISS JESSEL. How do you know?

QUINT. Because they've told me.

MISS JESSEL. The children have told you their dreams?

QUINT. Don't they tell you their dreams?

MISS JESSEL. No. They don't.

QUINT. Oh. I thought they might. I know they're reasonably fond of you. They've told me so. And I have no particular cause to suspect they would lie to me about a thing like that. They are, generally speaking, as far as I can tell, relatively truthful children, most of the time, and I think I can say without hesitation that the children are genuinely fond of you. I have absolute confidence in saying that.

MISS JESSEL. Just what are the children's bad dreams about?

QUINT. India. The children have dreams about India. The Punjab. The Ganges. Bombay and Nagpur. Mosquito nets draped over the corpses of dead Europeans. The rivers are brown and full of dead oxen. Snakes in the reeds. Crumbling temples. Elephants. Water buffalo. Camels mating. Crocodiles waddling lightning quick up the river bank to snatch unsuspecting infants in their jaws. Barefoot, haunted people in the narrow streets of Poona. Gorgeous dark-eyed women with somewhat annoying accents. A cacophany of Bengali, Hindustani, and Urdu. In the children's dreams, their parents are dying, their faces pasty and rotting. At night they come to look in the windows, trickles of blood running out the corners of their mouths. In their dreams the children wander the corridors of labyrinthine temples while snakes crawl up carvings of seven-breasted, twelve-armed dancing goddesses, and their parents lie naked in their beds, sweating from tropical fever, and hallucinating about Wembley.

(Pause.)

MISS JESSEL. I see.

QUINT. Whereas I, on the other hand, merely dream about you. Except now and then I also dream that somebody is looking in the windows. Outside looking in. And then, in my dream, I see that the face of that person is my face. I am the one who is outside looking in the windows, in my dream. And do you know what I see, Miss Jessel, when I'm looking in the windows, in my dream?

MISS JESSEL. I have no idea.

QUINT. Two naked figures, straining together in the darkness.

*(Pause. **MISS JESSEL** looks at him. Sound of a ticking clock as lights fade on her and **QUINT** moves downstage towards a wooden chair.)*

3

(QUINT sits on a wooden chair, polishing a pair of boots, speaking downstage to the invisible Miles. The MASTER is still drinking in his chair, and MISS JESSEL has seated herself upstage, also out of the light, doing a bit of needlepoint.)

QUINT. Oh, cheer up, young Master Miles. I know what it's like to be a boy. I do. You may not believe this, but I was a boy once, myself. Oh, yes. I can produce witnesses to verify this claim, if necessary. Even your uncle was a boy once. And in many respects, come to think of it, he still is. I lost my parents, too, at an early age. Mother was an actress, and a part time peach vendor. Father was a picture on the piano. Looked rather like Bonnie Prince Charlie, except of course he wasn't Scotch. Mother drank Scotch. She was a lovely woman, had many friends. She did more entertaining back-stage than she did onstage. I remember as a small child listening to her entertaining the Prince of Wales behind a screen. That woman was talented. She could have sung grand opera. Your grandfather was a good friend of hers. In her last months she grew uncharacteristically plump, rather like a Christmas turkey, cried a great deal, then took a midwinter dip in the Thames and sucked in rather too much cold water. Saw her in the coffin, perhaps her best performance, a wonderful stillness, something she never managed to achieve in life. Hell is memory. But, lucky for me, your grandfather took me under his wing, brought me to Bly, made me a stable boy – oh, I could tell you such stories about horse shit – and then, in the course of time, his eldest son's valet. Your uncle. So I knew them both, your uncle and your father. And your mother. I was proud to serve them all. And now here I am with you. So, do you know what the moral of that sad story is, young Master Miles? The moral of that story is, having a dead mother may actually turn out to be a spot of

good luck. So, cheer up, and tomorrow we'll go fishing in the lake. And if you're a very good boy, perhaps
we'll use your little sister for bait. Won't that be fun?

*(He spits on the boot, and gives it one last bit of rather
violent polishing as the light fades on him.)*

4

(Lights up on **MISS JESSEL** *doing her needlepoint in the parlor.* **QUINT** *goes upstage past her to deposit the boots in a closet.)*

QUINT. Ah, Miss Jessel. There you are, busy impaling an innocent, helpless piece of fabric with a long, sharp needle. Woman's work.

MISS JESSEL. Mr Quint, may I have a word with you?

QUINT. Why, certainly, Miss Jessel. What word would you like? Jackboots is a good word. Hurdy-gurdy. Glockenspiel. Lugubrious.

MISS JESSEL. I am a bit concerned, Mr Quint.

QUINT. Is this about Mrs Grose passing gas at the dinner table? I've tried to speak to her about it on several occasions, but there just seems to be no really satisfactory way of approaching the subject.

MISS JESSEL. It is not about Mrs Grose.

QUINT. Don't tell me we have rats again. I thought I could hear something scurrying up and down the main staircase in the middle of the night, but I rather hoped it was just the children. We had a tomcat once but they ate him. Not the children, the rats.

MISS JESSEL. I am not concerned about rats. I am concerned about the children.

QUINT. Well, of course. The rats can take care of themselves. But the children require constant discouragement.

MISS JESSEL. Mr Quint, I am concerned about your influence upon the children.

QUINT. My influence?

MISS JESSEL. Yes.

QUINT. Upon the children?

MISS JESSEL. Yes.

QUINT. I have influence upon the children? How extraordinary. I was entirely unaware that I had any influence whatsoever upon anything. But to have actually influenced children, especially these children, dear little Max and Dora, is beyond my wildest dreams.

MISS JESSEL. What I am trying to say, Mr Quint, is that it has come to my attention that you have been spending an extraordinary amount of time with the children.

QUINT. I have not been spending an extraordinary amount of time with the children, Miss Jessel. The children, however, have been spending an extraordinary amount of time with me. At least, Max has. Miles. That's it. Miles. Rhymes with piles. He follows me around like a duck without a mother.

MISS JESSEL. He seems to be uncommonly fond of you, Mr Quint, and I can't, for the life of me, imagine why.

QUINT. Well, we can't have that, can we? We can't have the children growing fond of us. No, that would be a catastrophe rivalling the decline and fall of the Roman Empire, wouldn't it? That these children could actually become fond of anybody, especially the hired help, is shocking beyond words. If they don't positively detest us, clearly we are not doing our job.

MISS JESSEL. I do not mind the children becoming fond of you, Mr Quint, within respectable parameters. But I feel that the danger exists –

QUINT. Yes? What? What do you feel, Miss Jessel?

MISS JESSEL. I feel that there is some danger –

QUINT. What danger? What danger exists, Miss Jessel? What danger do you feel in your immediate proximity?

MISS JESSEL. The danger that you are becoming somewhat too familiar with the children.

QUINT. Familiar. You believe I am too familiar with the children?

MISS JESSEL. I believe you are too familiar with everybody. My particular concern at the moment, however, is with the children.

QUINT. Do you believe I am too familiar with you, Miss Jessel?

MISS JESSEL. Yes. I do.

QUINT. And in exactly what respect am I too familiar with you?

MISS JESSEL. In your words. And in your manners.

QUINT. What manners? I haven't any manners.

MISS JESSEL. Exactly my point.

QUINT. But that's part of my charm, Miss Jessel. The Master himself has said that I am a very charming fellow. Are you calling the Master a liar?

MISS JESSEL. Certainly not.

QUINT. Then you agree that I am charming?

MISS JESSEL. Perhaps to some people in some circumstances you are charming. But I do not think you should be charming the children.

QUINT. You think there is some danger in the children being charmed? Do you think I am going to cast some sort of evil spell upon the children, is that what you're saying?

MISS JESSEL. No, that is not what I'm saying.

QUINT. Then what exactly are you saying, Miss Jessel? Because I rather got the impression that you found me charming.

MISS JESSEL. My feelings are not the point here, Mr Quint.

QUINT. Then what is the point?

MISS JESSEL. The children are the point.

QUINT. Do you have some recollection, Miss Jessel, of the state of mind of these children when they first arrived here?

MISS JESSEL. Of course I do.

QUINT. How would you describe it?

MISS JESSEL. They were very sad, of course. They had just lost both their parents and their entire world, and been packed off to a strange place.

QUINT. A very strange place, Miss Jessel. And what would you say is the children's state of mind now? Do they seem happier to you?

MISS JESSEL. Well, yes. Quite a bit happier.

QUINT. Then what exactly do you believe I've done to them that's so terrible?

MISS JESSEL. You talk to them.

QUINT. I talk to them? Well, how shameful. And what dire effect does my talking to them have upon these poor unfortunate children? Does it make them cry?

MISS JESSEL. No. It doesn't make them cry.

QUINT. Well, what does it make them do, then, Miss Jessel? Does it make them laugh?

MISS JESSEL. Yes. Often it makes them laugh, but –

QUINT. The children are sad, and I talk to them, and then they laugh, and therefore I am a terrible influence upon the children? Is that your argument, Miss Jessel?

MISS JESSEL. Could you just possibly try to be a bit less familiar with them? Could you just try and watch what you say to them? They are children, and can't be expected to understand when you are joking and when you are not.

QUINT. Unlike you, Miss Jessel?

MISS JESSEL. I did not mean to offend you, Mr Quint.

QUINT. I will tell you about these children, Miss Jessel. These children, on the whole, are rather interesting people. Perhaps you perceive it to be your job to make certain they get over that as soon as possible and become good little upper class cretins, but if that is the case, you must do that yourself. I am not prepared to assist you in that endeavor. And may I suggest, while we are on the subject of the children, that if you could possibly bring yourself to be just a bit more familiar with the children, Miss Jessel, perhaps they would also find you charming. And if you have any further complaints about the way I conduct myself with the children or for that matter with you, then I urge you to take your concerns up with the Master at the earliest opportunity. With any luck at all, you could get me sacked, and then the children would no doubt be in very little danger of ever being tempted to laugh at anything at all. Now if you will excuse me, Miss Jessel, I think it's time for me to go out to the lake and teach the children how to worship the Devil.

(He goes. **MISS JESSEL** *stands there. The light fades on her.)*

5

(Sound of a ticking clock. Lights up on the **MASTER**, *still seated in his chair before the fire, but now at Bly.* **MISS JESSEL** *brings flowers over in a vase and puts them on the table by the chair as the* **MASTER** *speaks, then sits down on the love seat.* **QUINT** *stands quietly in the upstage darkness, watching. Night.)*

MASTER. So, how have things been going here at Bly?

MISS JESSEL. Quite well, actually.

MASTER. No complaints?

MISS JESSEL. None that come to mind.

MASTER. Children doing well?

MISS JESSEL. Very well.

MASTER. They seem to have cheered up quite a bit.

MISS JESSEL. They are angels.

MASTER. Good. I'm glad to hear it. Mrs Grose been behaving herself, has she?

MISS JESSEL. As far as I know.

MASTER. Not getting into the cooking sherry?

MISS JESSEL. Not that I've noticed.

MASTER. Splendid. How is Quint?

MISS JESSEL. How is Quint?

MASTER. Yes. How are you and Quint getting along?

MISS JESSEL. Fine.

MASTER. No problems?

MISS JESSEL. Nothing I can recall.

MASTER. Has he been taking care of himself?

MISS JESSEL. I don't know what you mean.

MASTER. He's not well, you know.

MISS JESSEL. Isn't he?

MASTER. No. Not well at all. He hasn't been going out all hours of the night, tramping through the wet grass to the pub in the village, has he?

MISS JESSEL. I don't know what Mr Quint does at night.

MASTER. The children seem to like him.

MISS JESSEL. The children are fascinated by him.

MASTER. I thought they might be. He has the same power over animals. Horses adore him. Cats just can't get enough of him. Sheep follow him around. And women simply love him to death. Now, why do you suppose that is?

MISS JESSEL. I have no idea. I'm allergic to cats, myself.

MASTER. But Quint is a rather interesting fellow, don't you think?

MISS JESSEL. Interesting in what way?

MASTER. He sees things.

MISS JESSEL. What things?

MASTER. One doesn't exactly know. Because one doesn't necessarily see them one's self. Until Quint sees them. And then one begins seeing them, too. It's quite extraordinary, really.

(Pause.)

You're looking well. Quite beautiful, in fact. A bit pale, perhaps, but on you it looks good. You have always been beautiful.

(Pause.)

Quint looks like the Devil.

(Pause.)

I've been thinking about you.

(Pause.)

MISS JESSEL. Have you?

(Pause.)

QUINT. *(Stepping into the light.)* Excuse me, sir. Will you be needing anything else tonight, sir?

MASTER. No, Quint. I'm fine, thank you.

QUINT. More liquor, sir?

MASTER. I have plenty of liquor, thank you.

QUINT. Would Miss Jessel like anything?

MISS JESSEL. I'm fine, Quint, thank you.

MASTER. That will be all for tonight, Quint. Good night.

QUINT. Good night, sir. Good night, Miss Jessel.

MISS JESSEL. Good night.

*(Pause. **QUINT** doesn't move.)*

MASTER. Is there something else, Quint?

QUINT. No, sir.

MASTER. Good night, then.

QUINT. Yes. Good night.

*(He looks at **MISS JESSEL**.)*

Would you like to be awakened at any particular time, sir?

MASTER. No. No thank you, Quint. I am generally awakened, when in the country, by the crowing of the cock. As you well know.

QUINT. But I am correct in assuming, am I not, sir, that your intention is to be leaving early in the morning?

MASTER. Leaving? Whatever gave you that idea, Quint?

QUINT. You told me so yourself, sir.

MASTER. Did I?

QUINT. Yes, sir. You did.

MASTER. Well, no. I think perhaps I'll stay on one more day, at least, Quint. I'll let you know in the morning, all right? That won't inconvenience you too much, will it, Quint? Not knowing for certain?

QUINT. No, sir. Very good, sir.

(Pause.)

Good night, sir.

MASTER. Good night, Quint.

*(Pause. **QUINT** glances briefly at **MISS JESSEL**, then turns and goes.)*

Odd fellow, isn't he?

MISS JESSEL. Is he? I hadn't noticed.

(Lights fade on them. Sound of the ticking clock.)

6

(Lights up on **QUINT***, who sits down left in the merest suggestion of a small row boat, fishing on the lake with a rather crude fishing pole consisting of a piece of twine tied to the end of a cut branch and dangling into the darkness of the lake downstage before him, as* **MISS JESSEL** *moves to the foot of the staircase and sits there in the dark, and the* **MASTER** *remains in his chair.)*

QUINT. Now, Miles, I know that women can be infuriating on occasion, but we must never lose our temper with our little sister, but always be gentle and patient with her, and make allowances for her, because when she grows up, she will be a woman, and women are not like us, or rather, while they are often not like us when we expect them to be like us, they are sometimes like us when we don't expect them to be like us, and sometimes they make us very, very happy, for perhaps as much as five or ten minutes at a stretch, and also very, very sad, for periods usually not exceeding sixty or seventy years at the most, and if we are very lucky little fellows, now and then they will agree to pretend that they love us, through no inherent virtue of our own, at least for a time, while it's convenient for them, at any rate, and then, eventually, in the course of time, much like the black widow spider, they kill us and devour us. Unless of course we kill them first, but that is not playing fair, you see, Miles, because we are much bigger and stronger than they are, so we must, as a point of honor, allow them to murder us, unless of course we are members of the aristocracy, or at least have money, in which case we get to murder them. The important thing to remember about a woman, Miles, is that you must forget her, and go on about your business, which is, unfortunately, entirely impossible. Oh, look. I believe I've actually caught something.

(The light fades on **QUINT** *as the* **MASTER** *finishes his drink, gets up, and disappears into the darkness.)*

7

(Sound of a ticking clock. Lights up on **MISS JESSEL,**
sitting on the steps at the foot of the staircase. **QUINT**
moves into the light from behind her, stops, looks at her.)

QUINT. You are brooding, Miss Jessel.

MISS JESSEL. God, you startled me.

QUINT. You are not unlike a figure out of Romance, brooding there. Miss Jessel broods upon the staircase. At
the foot of the staircase, Miss Jessel sits brooding. The
beautiful and mysterious Miss Jessel sat brooding at
the foot of the staircase one dark night while bats flut-
tered at the windows, and rooks cawed and flapped
above the ancient tower. By the foot of the staircase
she sat down and wept, Miss Jessel the lily maid of Bly.

MISS JESSEL. Must you forever be creeping up on me like
some horrible spider?

QUINT. I am the Caretaker of Bly, Miss Jessel. I consider it
my solemn duty to lurk about, spying upon the hired
help.

MISS JESSEL. Have you been drinking?

QUINT. Drinking? Me? I? The Caretaker of Bly drinking?
The former valet to the Master of Bly allowing unclean
spirits to enter into the sacred orifice of his mouth?
Shame on you for thinking such a thing.

MISS JESSEL. I take it that means yes.

QUINT. *(Taking out a flask and unscrewing the cap.)* I drink
only for medicinal purposes. I am not well, you know.

(He sits down beside her on the steps.)

Do you want some? No? Well, don't say I didn't make
the offer. Couple of good snorts now and then might
loosen you up a little. That is, if you still need loosen-
ing up, after the Master's visit.

(He drinks.)

MISS JESSEL. I hope you have not been drinking around the
children.

QUINT. The Master drinks around the children.

MISS JESSEL. You are not the Master.

QUINT. No. I am not the Master. I must try and keep that in mind. And I have no doubt that you have taken advantage of his recent visit to acquaint the Master of Bly with my drinking habits. No doubt you have given him a careful report of all my multitudinous sins in lurid and more or less grammatically correct detail.

MISS JESSEL. I might well have spoken to him in some detail of your drinking habits and of a number of other somewhat questionable elements in your character and general behavior. But, as it happens, I did not.

QUINT. Well, that was magnanimous of you. I don't wish to shock you, Miss Jessel, but the Master of Bly knows that his former valet, Peter Quint, drinks. The Master of Bly has spent many an hour drinking and carousing in the company of his former valet, the somewhat questionable Peter Quint. In fact, on one particularly memorable occasion, the somewhat questionable Peter Quint had the tremendous honor of observing the Master of Bly consume enough liquor to incapacitate a Welsh regiment and then vomit repeatedly and with prodigious violence directly into the pot of Lady Ashburnham's prize-winning aspidistra.

MISS JESSEL. Will you please just go away and leave me alone?

QUINT. You think the children don't know what's going on, but they know, Miss Jessel.

MISS JESSEL. They know what?

QUINT. They know a great deal more than it makes you comfortable to believe they know. I have been making a careful study of these children, as one would study a rare species of Sumatran marmoset, and I have discovered that they possess remarkable powers. They see things.

MISS JESSEL. What things?

QUINT. They can see in the dark.

MISS JESSEL. No they can't.

QUINT. Oh, yes. They creep about the house at night in the dark, entirely without benefit of candles. They put glasses to bedroom doors and listen. They peep in keyholes. They have skeleton keys which they insert in locks and turn ever so carefully so they can scuttle like crabs into rooms at night and watch whatever you do. The very most private things you do. They are always watching. Their little wide eyes take in everything. They are quite capable of detecting even microsopic blemishes in your bosom. They know you intimately.

MISS JESSEL. They don't know me at all, and neither do you.

QUINT. Oh, we all know you, Miss Jessel.

MISS JESSEL. You don't know me.

QUINT. I know you. I have known you for some time. I know you now. And in the future, I hope to know you even better. I think I shall know you best of all when I am dead. And of course, the Master knows you.

(Pause.)

MISS JESSEL. You're a horrible, horrible man.

QUINT. But I'm yours.

MISS JESSEL. You're not mine.

QUINT. But, if I'm not yours, then whose am I?

MISS JESSEL. No doubt some wretched, ignorant village sluts at the pub.

QUINT. Village sluts? What do you know about village sluts? You know nothing at all about village sluts. You're a great lady.

MISS JESSEL. I'm a governess in a country house, no more and no less, and I should like very much to be left alone now.

QUINT. You long to be in London, don't you?

MISS JESSEL. What would I do in London?

QUINT. You'd be closer to him there.

MISS JESSEL. I don't know what you're talking about.

QUINT. Time passes and you do not see him. Trapped here in the country. Hell among the dragon flies. He comes and you are so excited, and then he goes and you're abandoned once again. And yet there is a kind of weird and mystical fascination comes with such rural isolation, don't you think? The quiet. The ticking of the clocks. The dismal chattering of the birds. The caw of the rooks circling aimlessly above the crumbling towers. Do you still have hopes he will come one day and carry you off to London?

MISS JESSEL. I can't go to London. I've got the children.

QUINT. Well, of course I meant with the children. Did you think I meant he would come and take you to London without the children?

MISS JESSEL. I don't know what you meant. I never know what you mean.

QUINT. You always know what I mean.

MISS JESSEL. You are not a gentleman.

QUINT. I am not a gentleman.

MISS JESSEL. And I have growing fears that you are corrupting the children.

QUINT. I am teaching the children about life.

MISS JESSEL. Oh, I see. And is that what you think you're doing by tormenting me day and night? Are you teaching me about life?

QUINT. I think the Master has already taught you about life.

MISS JESSEL. Get away from me. You're disgusting.

QUINT. And yet disgusting as I am, still you did not speak ill of me to the Master when you might have. Miss Jessel, if you find me so disgusting, then why did you not speak ill of me to the Master?

MISS JESSEL. Because I pity you.

QUINT. You pity me? You pity the Caretaker of Bly?

MISS JESSEL. Yes. I do.

QUINT. And why exactly do you pity me?

MISS JESSEL. Because you're so unhappy.

QUINT. Am I? Am I unhappy?

MISS JESSEL. You're extremely unhappy.

QUINT. Why am I unhappy?

MISS JESSEL. You're ill, for one thing. And for another, you're a desperately lonely man.

QUINT. Lonely? The Caretaker of Bly is lonely? Peter Quint is lonely? Ask among your good friends the village sluts if you seek to find out the truth about Peter Quint's alleged loneliness. Peter Quint has left a trail of broken sluts draped all up and down the cobbles of the village streets and alleys. Peter Quint has had his pick of the ripest and most distinguished village sluts in all of Essex. I do believe Miss Jessel is seeing her own unhappiness reflected in the eyes of Peter Quint. Miss Jessel is brooding at the foot of the staircase because she has been once again most cruelly abandoned by the Master of Bly. Miss Jessel is grieving for her wayward upperclass demon lover.

(She slaps him, very hard, across the face, with enough force to knock him backwards off the steps. He gets up, grabs her by the shoulders and presses her against the steps.)

Now is that any way to treat poor, sick, lonely Peter Quint, who deserves every ounce of pity the pathetic and repeatedly deflowered village slut Miss Jessel can muster for him?

MISS JESSEL. Take your hands off me.

QUINT. She patronizes me and pities me and looks down her aristocratic nose at me and all the while the governess is rutting for all she's worth all night naked with the Master in his big soft canopy bed, moaning and whimpering and sobbing in her exquisite degradation. Now that is pitiful. That is a genuinely pitiful thing.

MISS JESSEL. Let go of me or I'll cry out for help.

QUINT. Yes, I think you should cry out for help. I think you should scream like a banshee, and wake the children with your bellowing. I think we should get that great stupid cow Mrs Grose out here gaping at us with one child huddled staring wide-eyed under each of her floppy pork roast arms. Now that will give them nightmares. That will teach them about life. Their sweet pretty governess Miss Jessel found shrieking and deranged on the staircase in the middle of the night while poor, lonely Peter Quint attempts to comfort her. Yes, let's wake up the children, by all means.

MISS JESSEL. You're a monster.

QUINT. I am a monster, yes. I am a monster. You have given yourself like a common Whitechapel whore to our employer just down the hall from where his dead brother's children sleep, the children of your dead friend their mother – while they are having nightmares about India their beloved governess is down the hall copulating like monkeys with their uncle, but I am a monster because I am not a gentleman, I must take the long walk down the avenue of beech trees to the pub to find my consolation in the swelling breasts of pathetic and ignorant village girls, but dear Miss Jessel, sweet Miss Jessel, kind, innocent, tender Miss Jessel, who teaches the children bad French and worse Latin, fornicates with their uncle like a couple of goats not forty feet away from where they lie in their beds, yet I am a monster. I am a monster.

MISS JESSEL. What do you want from me? What do you want from me?

QUINT. What do I want from you? What does the monster Peter Quint want from the beautiful governess and part time prostitute Miss Jessel? What do I want from you? Not your pity. Not your pity.

(He lets her go and walks away. She sits on the steps and sobs, great, terrible, heart-rending sobs. A moment. He steps back into the light. He watches her sobbing there. When he speaks again, his voice is gentle.)

He does not mean to hurt you. He is not a cruel man.

He simply – he fears attachments. He was quite fond of his brother, you know. Took good care of him when the old man died. They grew up here, in this place. It was a cold place, even then. He is simply incapable of love. And for some reason we find such people attractive. I don't know why. Our fascination with our own death, perhaps. We look into the eyes of the beloved and see our own death reflected back to us. Love is a terrible, dark mirror. This house is full of mirrors. I hate this house.

(Pause.)

Miss Jessel.

MISS JESSEL. Go away. Please just go away and leave me alone.

QUINT. I can't. I can't go away and I can't leave you alone. I can't leave you alone because I am a monster. I can't go away because I have nowhere else to go. And because of the children. They are really our children, now, you know, yours and mine. Their parents are scattered ashes in the Ganges. Their uncle doesn't want to think about them. Mrs Grose is a great stupid farting cow. So you and I are all they have, you see. I can't leave you alone because you are the mother of our children, as it were. And because I can still feel your arms in the palms of my hands. Your body against mine. I can smell your hair.

MISS JESSEL. Please.

QUINT. I make you suffer because the thought of you is absolute torture to me, and I can't stop thinking of you. Everything here is you.

MISS JESSEL. Please.

QUINT. I make you suffer because you are the mistress of my own particular Hell. You are the face I see in my dark mirror.

(He gets down on his knees beside her.)

MISS JESSEL. Please.

QUINT. I am not a gentleman.

MISS JESSEL. Don't.

QUINT. I am only a servant.

MISS JESSEL. If you touch me, I'll scream.

QUINT. I am only a servant.

(He rests his forehead upon her thigh.)

And I am not well. I am not well at all. Not at all.

(A moment. She touches his hair. The light fades on them and goes out.)

8

(Sound of a ticking clock. Lights up on the wooden chair. **MISS JESSEL** *moves into the light and sits, holding a rag doll onto which she is sewing a button eye.)*

MISS JESSEL. Don't be sad, Flora, because Miles has torn the eyes off your dolly. Miss Jessel will sew on new eyes for her. The eyes, you know, Flora, are the windows of the soul. We use our eyes for important things like looking. It is with our eyes that we look in the mirror. And of course the girl we see in the mirror has eyes as well, and she looks back at us. She is our reflection, and our double. She sees everything we do. She is like us, but she lives behind the looking glass and does the opposite of what we are. Sometimes I wish I could be her, live in her world. I know that she must be happy there, in the mirror, although sometimes she looks very sad. I think that when I am gone away, she will be here to take care of you, and she will look in the mirror and see somebody else looking back at her. When I look at you, I see your mother. Your mother was such a pretty girl. She and I used to sometimes sleep in the same bed, when we were little girls, and I would hold her in my arms and watch her sleep. And what do you see when you look in the mirror, my dear? A very pretty girl. A very pretty girl indeed, who will make all the men cry one day. So, Flora, remember, if men pluck out your eyes, just come to me, and I will sew them on again for you. I will sew them on again, so you can see.

(She finishes. Sits the doll on her lap, facing out. The button eyes of the doll look out into the darkness with **MISS JESSEL.** *The light fades on her and goes out.)*

9

(Sound of birds. Lights up on **MISS JESSEL***, who has left the doll sitting on the chair and moved down center to stand at the shore of the lake, which is the edge of the stage, looking out at the water.* **QUINT** *steps from the darkness into the upstage edge of the light and watches her.)*

MISS JESSEL. We are getting deep into the autumn now.

QUINT. Yes.

MISS JESSEL. I love this lake. I can come and stare into it for hours. It's haunted, you know. But everything here is haunted. It's like a mirror. There is somebody looking out at me. I don't know who it is. I feel as if I'm always being watched.

QUINT. You are. You are always being watched.

(He moves downstage towards her and touches her back.)

MISS JESSEL. *(Stepping away from his touch.)* It will be dark soon. I should go back. The children will be wondering where I've gotten to.

QUINT. The children will be fine. I've taught them how to amuse themselves.

MISS JESSEL. Have you?

QUINT. Tell me what's wrong.

MISS JESSEL. Do you ever feel that you are drowning?

QUINT. Now and then I can't breathe.

MISS JESSEL. The water is a perfect mirror. I feel sometimes that I am drowning in the mirror.

QUINT. Just close your eyes and tell yourself it isn't real.

MISS JESSEL. I've tried that. It doesn't seem to work for me.

(Pause.)

You've been saying odd things to the children.

QUINT. Have I? What kind of things?

MISS JESSEL. Odd things. You've been teaching them things.

QUINT. What things?

MISS JESSEL. I don't think you should do that.

QUINT. I can't prevent them from learning, if they want to learn. You're their teacher. That's your job.

MISS JESSEL. But the way you treat them. You treat them –

QUINT. What? Badly? Do I treat them badly?

MISS JESSEL. You treat them as if they were adults.

QUINT. I treat them as my equals.

MISS JESSEL. But that's just it. They are not your equals.

QUINT. Because I am not a gentleman.

MISS JESSEL. Because you are not a child.

QUINT. I have great respect for these children. I would not do them the indignity of lying to them.

MISS JESSEL. But Mrs Grose has noticed.

QUINT. Noticed what?

MISS JESSEL. That something is not right.

QUINT. What is not right?

MISS JESSEL. The children. The children are too wise. It's not normal.

QUINT. Nothing worth doing is normal.

(*Pause.*)

MISS JESSEL. I have to go.

QUINT. Why have you been avoiding me?

MISS JESSEL. I really need to get back. I –

QUINT. (*Getting in her way.*) Tell me why you've been avoiding me. We must speak of this. You and I must speak of this.

MISS JESSEL. (*Moving nervously away from him.*) I don't wish to speak of it. What has happened between us must stop now. Do you understand? From this moment on, it must stop. It must never happen again. It was an aberration. And it is wrong. You know that it's wrong. I was very unhappy, and you were very unhappy, and we came together that night, and we comforted one another. And we have comforted one another on many nights since. And I treasure that. I genuinely treasure that comfort. I cannot emphasize enough how grateful I am, that in my despair, you were there to comfort me. But it must never happen again. We must forget about it now.

QUINT. Forget.

MISS JESSEL. Yes. Forget. We must forget.

QUINT. As if forgetting were an exercise of will.

MISS JESSEL. I can't bear to argue with you about this. If you have any real feelings for me –

QUINT. If I have any real feelings for you? As opposed to what? As opposed to the imaginary feelings I have for you? Do you think that I have come here to impersonate a lover? Do you think I am a character in a book? A painted figure upon a stage?

MISS JESSEL. I am merely attempting to communicate to you what you must already know as well as I, that our situation is impossible.

QUINT. Of course it's impossible. Everything that matters is impossible. Everything real is impossible.

MISS JESSEL. Then if you agree that our situation is impossible, surely you must understand that –

(He puts his hands on her arms from behind. She stiffens, but doesn't pull away.)

Don't touch me. Please. You must not touch me. You have never touched me.

QUINT. I have touched you. I have touched every part of you. I have kissed every part of you. I have kissed your naked back. I have kissed your naked thighs. I have copulated with you naked in the firelight.

MISS JESSEL. You have done no such thing. It is entirely imaginary.

QUINT. Shall I describe your breasts for you? I have memorized your breasts in the firelight.

MISS JESSEL. Nothing has happened between us.

QUINT. Shall I describe the sound you make, the sudden intake of your breath when I enter you?

(Running the palms of his hands up and down her arms from behind.)

MISS JESSEL. It never happened. It never happened.

QUINT. Do you mean to tell me I have imagined your arms? The perfect shape and contour of your arms, the flesh of your arms? Has this all been a drunken hallucination? Is that what you are telling me?

(He is kissing her hair.)

MISS JESSEL. The children will see us.

QUINT. It will be an excellent education for them in the power of imagination.

(He kisses the back of her neck.)

Of course, on the other hand, perhaps you are right. Perhaps I am imagining this. For it's entirely too pleasurable to be real. Am I imagining you entirely, Miss Jessel?

(He is kissing her shoulders.)

MISS JESSEL. Yes. I am entirely imaginary. This is not happening. The truth is, you are not well at all. In fact, I fear you are quite mad.

QUINT. *(Kissing her arms.)* I am quite mad.

MISS JESSEL. And there is a part of your brain which knows that you are mad. And that is the part which believes that it is speaking now to that impossible figment of your imagination to which you believe you are making love. We are no more real than characters in a book, you and I.

QUINT. *(Running his hands along her stomach and up between her breasts from behind.)* Characters in a book.

MISS JESSEL. This is fantasy. It is entirely fantasy. You are dreaming this. This is your loneliness and your unhappiness and your sickness and your ultimate madness. This is not happening at all. And we must stop before the children see.

QUINT. If this is a dream then what does it matter if the children see?

MISS JESSEL. It matters because there are some things children should not see even in their dreams.

QUINT. *(Pulling her down from behind so that she is sitting on the ground, and he is on his knees, bending over her from behind, kissing her forehead from above.)* I would advise you to brace yourself, Miss Jessel, because this figment of my imagination is now going to make desperate love to the governess in her dream.

MISS JESSEL. No. You can't.

QUINT. I can and I have and I will again forever. You can't stop me because I am an entirely imaginary personage, and I am not a gentleman.

MISS JESSEL. You can't, because somebody is watching us, and it is not the children. There is somebody on the other side of the water.

QUINT. *(Kissing her cheeks and her eyes.)* Is it him? Is he watching? Has he come back to watch us?

MISS JESSEL. I think it is a woman.

QUINT. Is it that dirty-minded busybody Mrs Grose? Well, this will give her something to think about before she goes to sleep at night, won't it?

MISS JESSEL. No. It's a young woman. She's watching us. Look.

QUINT. *(Kissing her throat.)* I don't see anybody.

MISS JESSEL. You're not looking. She is watching us. She is watching us. I think it is the woman in the mirror.

QUINT. *(Kissing her breasts.)* You have seen nobody in the mirror.

MISS JESSEL. It is the other governess.

QUINT. *(Kissing her stomach.)* What other governess? You are the governess. There is no other governess.

MISS JESSEL. It is the governess in the mirror. It is the girl in the mirror.

QUINT. *(Kissing her thighs.)* There is nobody in the mirror. You and I have no reflection whatsoever.

MISS JESSEL. Because we are imaginary. Because we are dead.

QUINT. I don't care.

(He kisses up her body and lies on top of her.)

MISS JESSEL. We are dead people, and she is seeing us.

QUINT. She can look all she wants. I don't care.

(He is kissing her lips.)

MISS JESSEL. *(Holding her face away from him.)* Peter Quint. Look at me. Look at me.

(She holds his face so that he is looking directly into her eyes.)

What do you see when you look in my eyes? What do you see?

QUINT. When I look in your eyes I see my own death.

MISS JESSEL. Then why do you want me so?

QUINT. Because that is what love is.

MISS JESSEL. Listen to me. I do not love you. Do you understand? I do not love you.

QUINT. That's a lie.

MISS JESSEL. I do not love you. I love him. He is the only one I love or ever could love. I loved him before I knew you and I will love him after you are dead and I love him now, while your body is pressing against me, and when I close my eyes when you are making love to me, all the times you have made love to me, all through the strange, unreal summer, each time you have made love to me, I have thought of him. I have cried out for him. You are not loved, Peter Quint. Do you understand? You are not loved.

QUINT. I don't believe you.

MISS JESSEL. Yes you do. You know it. You've always known it.

QUINT. It doesn't matter what you say you feel. It only matters that we share the same nightmare.

MISS JESSEL. Peter, listen to me. Listen to me. If you love me, will you please do this one thing for me? Will you stop this now? Will you stop it now before it devours us both entirely?

QUINT. I can't.

> *(He buries his face in her hair.)*

I can't.

MISS JESSEL. There is something else.

QUINT. There is nothing else.

MISS JESSEL. There is something I must tell you.

QUINT. Nothing matters but this.

MISS JESSEL. I've received a communication.

QUINT. A communication? From the spirit world?

MISS JESSEL. From London.

> *(He raises his head and looks at her.)*

QUINT. A communication from London.

MISS JESSEL. The Master is arriving tomorrow.

QUINT. Is he?

MISS JESSEL. Yes. He is.

QUINT. Tomorrow?

MISS JESSEL. Yes. Tomorrow.

QUINT. He's informed you but not me?

MISS JESSEL. He's written to me. He's arriving tomorrow.

QUINT. He's given us one day's notice?

MISS JESSEL. No. The message came last week. I just – I didn't want to tell you. I didn't want to spoil this.

QUINT. Spoil what?

MISS JESSEL. This. This hallucination. I wanted it to last just a bit longer. But it can't, any more. This is the end of it.

QUINT. Why?

MISS JESSEL. What do you mean, why?

QUINT. Why is he coming now?

MISS JESSEL. Why shouldn't he come? It's his house. He can come any time he wants to.

QUINT. Of course he can. What was I thinking? Everything here belongs to him, doesn't it?

> *(She looks at him.)*

Doesn't it?

MISS JESSEL. We should go back now.

QUINT. Yes.

MISS JESSEL. It's getting cold. You'll catch a chill. You are not well.

QUINT. Yes. I am not well.

(They don't move. Sound of rooks cawing. Lights fade on them and go out. End of Act One.)

ACT TWO

10

*(Sound of a ticking clock. Night. Lights up slowly on
the* MASTER, QUINT *and* MISS JESSEL, *sitting before the
fire at Bly, the* MASTER *in his chair, drinking,* QUINT
and MISS JESSEL *on opposite ends of the love seat,* MISS
JESSEL *nearest the* MASTER.*)*

MASTER. Well, I must say, I'm pleased that everything here
appears to be going so well.

QUINT. Thank you, sir.

MASTER. The children are positively glowing with happiness. I hope they're not stupid. Are they stupid?

QUINT. They are very bright children.

MASTER. Are they?

MISS JESSEL. Extremely bright.

MASTER. Both of them?

MISS JESSEL. Oh, yes.

MASTER. Hmm. I can't imagine where they get that. My
brother was a dear fellow, but he possessed about as
much brain matter as a brass door-knocker. Those we
send to India, to perpetuate the glory of the Empire,
where they read Kipling and raise peacocks, and die
of unspeakable diseases. Poor old Bob. Staggering
Bob, we used to call him. He was forever stumbling on
the rug and knocking over credenzas. He could never
quite get his balance. Unless he was drunk, of course.
Then he could walk the edge of the battlements like
the ghost of Hamlet's father, reciting Beowulf in the
original. At least, he said it was Beowulf. It sounded
like gibberish to me. But then, what doesn't? His wife
was awfully nice, though, wasn't she?

MISS JESSEL. Yes. She was.

MASTER. I still think often of my brother's wife. Especially when I look at little Dora.

MISS JESSEL. Flora.

MASTER. I don't know how you two do it.

QUINT. Do what, sir?

MASTER. Deal with children. The most horrifying thing I can think of, off hand, is being confronted by the trusting, jam-smeared face of a child. They want so very badly to idolize one, and yet just one slip, just one tiny slip, and they'll turn on you like a ferret in a chamber pot, and make you into a kind of jowl-slathering cacodemon in their minds. With children, it is all primitive mythology, all gods and demons, one or the other, no territory in-between. They are ruthless and pitiless, and they positively chill my blood. Their morbid attatchment to arcane rituals. Their insatiable hunger for love. Their instantaneous recognition of betrayal. I'd rather face a maniac with a hand ax.

(He drinks.)

But then, children are the consequence of marriage, which is an even more blood-chilling monstrosity to contemplate. Trapped in a coffin with the same hideous decaying bag of flesh for decades of an absolute, unrelenting hell of intimacy. Unless of course one is fortunate enough to die young. Did you ever think of marrying, Quint?

QUINT. Just once, sir.

MASTER. I'd strongly advise against it. My brother's marriage was not a happy one, I fear. The wife suffered greatly. I know that for a fact. And of course the children always sniff it out when there's trouble between the parents. My brother was a wonderful human being, very handy with a cricket bat, but he was not kind to that girl. And she was a thoroughly splendid girl. But of course, I don't have to tell you that, do I, Miss Jessel?

MISS JESSEL. No. You don't.

MASTER. We both knew her quite well, didn't we?

MISS JESSEL. Yes. We did.

MASTER. Intimately, in fact. We both knew my brother's wife quite intimately.

(*He drinks.*)

MISS JESSEL. I am feeling rather tired now. I believe I'll go up and look in on the children, and then be off to bed.

MASTER. Off to bed. Look in on the children and then off to bed. What a life.

MISS JESSEL. Good night.

MASTER. Good night, Miss Jessel. Sweet dreams.

(*She looks at* **QUINT**, *then goes. They both watch her walk upstage in the darkness. Pause.*)

QUINT. It's so good of you to honor us with a visit, sir.

MASTER. Well, I was passing by and it was raining. I've just made a little pilgrimage to Canterbury.

QUINT. Paying a call on the Archbishop, were you?

MASTER. Yes. As a matter of fact, I was.

QUINT. Did you make fun of his hat?

MASTER. Of course I did. But he didn't mind. He's a good sport.

QUINT. Do you drink with him?

MASTER. Yes. I've had a drink with the Archbishop, on one or two occasions.

QUINT. And on one or two occasions, you've had a drink with me.

MASTER. On more than one or two, Quint, I'm afraid. But I would never make fun of your hat.

(*He drinks.*)

So, you've been having a jolly good time of it, then, here at Bly, as the Caretaker of Bly, have you?

QUINT. I'm having a very good time of it here, sir, thank you.

MASTER. I'm glad to hear it. And is your health better?

QUINT. My health?

MASTER. I sent you here for your health, Quint. Is it better?

QUINT. Never felt better in my life, sir. I could run the high hurdles, if called upon. I'd enter myself in the English Derby, if they'd let me.

MASTER. That's good, Quint. I couldn't be more pleased to hear it. Because, frankly, you know, my initial impression, when I first laid eyes upon you, after our separation, was, as I believe I mentioned to Miss Jessel, my impression at the time was that you looked like the Devil.

QUINT. The Devil?

MASTER. That was my impression at the time.

QUINT. You were telling Miss Jessel I look like the Devil?

MASTER. It happened to come up. In conversation.

QUINT. Well, sir, I am not the Devil. One of his minions, perhaps.

MASTER. I didn't say you were the Devil, Quint. I said you looked like the Devil. I know you're not the Devil.

QUINT. How do you know, sir?

MASTER. How do I know?

QUINT. Yes. How do you know I'm not the Devil?

MASTER. Because the Devil is a friend of mine. I've just been having drinks with him and the Archibishop of Canterbury.

QUINT. I see. And they are good friends, are they? The Devil and the Archbishop of Canterbury?

MASTER. Oh, yes. They're members of the same club, you see. And of course they go fox hunting together in the autumn. Blood sports. God and the Devil both enjoy blood sports.

(Pause.)

So, do you think Miss Jessel is doing a good job? I mean with the children.

QUINT. The children worship her.

MASTER. I didn't ask you about the children's religion, Quint. I asked you if you thought Miss Jessel was doing a good job with them.

QUINT. Oh, she's doing a wonderful job, sir. She's an extraordinary woman. Miss Jessel is perhaps the most extraordinary woman with whom I've ever had the pleasure of being acquainted. But I don't have to tell you that, sir.

MASTER. No, you don't.

(Pause.)

Lovely girl, too. Just lovely. Excellent buttocks.

(Pause.)

I say, excellent buttocks. Yes? Quint? What's the matter, Quint? Not feeling well?

QUINT. Perhaps I am not well, sir.

MASTER. You're not? I thought you were entering the English Derby.

QUINT. The truth is, sir, I've been having bad dreams.

MASTER. Have you? Indigestion? Mrs Grose's mystery meat?

QUINT. I think perhaps this place has given me bad dreams.

MASTER. That's a shame, Quint. What do you dream about?

QUINT. Sometimes I'm walking in the cold. Coming home from the pub in the village. And the path is icy. It's a clear night. Full moon. But the moon has gone behind a cloud. It's quite late. I seem to have taken a wrong turn in the dark. And I have this sudden absolute knowledge that something is walking behind me.

MASTER. Really? And what is it? What's walking behind you, Quint, in your dream?

QUINT. I don't know. I expect at some point I shall find out.

MASTER. How will you find out?

QUINT. I'll turn around and look it directly in the eye.

MASTER. I see. And then what?

QUINT. Then I'm afraid I shall have to kill it.

(*Pause.*)

MASTER. Well, everybody is afraid, Quint.

QUINT. Are they?

MASTER. That's been my experience, at any rate.

QUINT. And what are you afraid of, sir? I mean, besides women and children?

MASTER. All men are afraid of women.

QUINT. Do you fear Miss Jessel?

MASTER. Miss Jessel – is a splendid girl.

QUINT. Yes. Spectacular buttocks.

MASTER. Yes. And perhaps it's not women themselves we fear so much as the power they have over us, potentially, if we're not careful. One fears most what one desires most, because it has the greatest power to do us injury, don't you think? What do you fear the most, Quint? Do you fear Miss Jessel most? Or me?

(*Pause.*)

QUINT. A man would be a fool not to fear Miss Jessel, sir.

(*Pause.*)

MASTER. Yes he would.

(*He drinks.*)

Been making any progress with her, Quint?

QUINT. Sir?

MASTER. I sense a certain – electricity in the room. When you and she are here together. In the same room. And it leads me to wonder, just for my own information, if you've been making any progress with her? Because, you know, Quint, I understand, if you are. I mean, I know what a ladies' man you are. I myself am also quite a ladies' man, so I understand perfectly if you find Miss Jessel quite irresistible. I find her quite irresistible myself. I have always been drawn to melancholy women. Of course, I'm also drawn to giggly, ridiculous women, and women who ride bareback at the circus. I am drawn to women with nicely shaped breasts. Not large ones, necessarily, just shapely. After all, we are not animals, we are English. Well, we are animals, but we are also English, so that should count for something, shouldn't it? And I love backs. The back of a woman, the line of the back, between the ribs, from the neck and shoulders down to the small of the back and then the buttocks. Oh, I love the buttocks of women, and their thighs, the backs of their thighs. I like a buxom wench, sturdy, but I am particularly drawn to the delicate, melancholy ones with great sad eyes, like Miss Jessel. She is quite an amazing young woman. Very accomplished, in her way. Piano fingers. I envy you, Quint, her regular company. I really do.

(Pause.)

Of course, if you're plowing her, I shall be forced to rip out your intestines and wrap them around your neck.

(Pause.)

But you wouldn't do that, would you, Quint? Because you know your place. When I describe you to my friends, as I do from time to time, I say, that Quint, now, there is a fellow who knows his place.

(Pause.)

QUINT. And do you know my place, sir?

MASTER. Of course I know your place. I am the one who puts you in your place. This is your place. Right here. This is it.

(Pause.)

I think we've had too much to drink, Quint.

QUINT. Have we?

MASTER. I believe we have. At any rate, I have. Yes, I think it's time for the Master of Bly to trundle himself on up the spiral staircase. I'm going up to bed, now.

(He gets up.)

QUINT. *(Getting up.)* Yes, sir. Up to bed. Will you be requiring any assistance, sir?

MASTER. Assistance?

QUINT. Yes, sir. I am, after all, still your valet, sir.

MASTER. You, Quint, are the Caretaker of Bly. That's what you are. And don't you ever forget it.

(He starts to go, then turns back briefly.)

You take care, Quint. Take care.

QUINT. I will, sir.

MASTER. *(Patting him three times heartily on the stomach.)* Good man. Good night, my friend.

QUINT. Good night, sir.

(He watches him walk away.)

Sir?

MASTER. *(Stopping.)* Yes, Quint?

QUINT. Will you be wanting your hot water bottle tonight?

MASTER. My hot water bottle?

QUINT. Yes, sir. To keep you warm in bed, sir.

MASTER. Thank you, Quint, but I don't think I shall be needing a hot water bottle tonight.

QUINT. It's a very cold night, sir.

MASTER. I know it's a cold night, Quint. But I'm sure I shall manage to find some way of keeping myself warm. Sweet dreams, Quint.

(He goes. Quint stands there, face dead. Lights fade on him and go out. Just the ticking of the clock.)

11

(Sound of the ticking clock. Night. Lights up on MISS
JESSEL, *sitting on a chair by a small lamp, holding the
rag doll in her lap.)*

MISS JESSEL. It was only a bad dream, Flora, and we must
not allow bad dreams to upset us too much. When I
was a girl I had many bad dreams. I dreamed something horrible lived under my bed and came up at
night to creep under the covers and lie on top of me
and smother me. I dreamed that something lived in
the closet and the door would creak open at mid-
night and a hideous spider creature with two red eyes
would look out at me. I dreamed that my father was
dead and I crawled up into the coffin so I could be
put in the tomb with him, and he reached up his cold,
dead hand and stroked my hair. I dreamed that I sat
naked and cold upon the top of a high tower, sobbing
and sobbing for my beloved, who had abandoned me.
I dreamed that I was lying at the bottom of a dark,
cold body of water, like a mirror, naked and shudder-
ing and lost there. I dreamed that a man crawled up
the side of the house and in the window of my room
at night to suck out my brains through a straw in my
ear. But you see, Flora, what a happy and well adjusted
young woman I have grown up into. So you must con-
quer your bad dreams too. Because your dreams really
can't hurt you, you know, as long as you always remember to make a great show of carefully nurturing your
indifference. It is always desire that kills, my love. It is
always desire that kills.

(She reaches over and turns out the lamp. Darkness.)

12

(Moonlight, eerie, blue. **MISS JESSEL** *making her way up the last steps to the top of the old tower. She stands looking out into the darkness. After a moment,* **QUINT** *steps out of the shadows behind her.)*

QUINT. You shouldn't stand so close to the edge.

MISS JESSEL. *(Startled, losing her balance for a brief moment.)* Oh.

QUINT. *(Calmly reaching out a hand to steady her.)* Did they not teach you that as a child, Miss Jessel? One who stands at the tower's edge is tempting fate. You might stumble, or become dizzy, or be distracted by the rooks circling above your head, or someone might come upon you unexpectedly and startle you, and you could fall. It's a terrible thing to fall, Miss Jessel.

MISS JESSEL. What are you doing up here?

QUINT. I'm concerned about you, Miss Jessel. You've not been eating well at all, ever since the Master left. Mrs Grose is worried. The children are worried. And I am absolutely beside myself. It's true. If you look closely, just to my left, you can actually see me there, beside myself, looking worried.

MISS JESSEL. Go away.

QUINT. I do hope he hasn't broken your heart again, Miss Jessel. That would be a shame.

MISS JESSEL. Don't torture me.

QUINT. Just what exactly did you think would happen? Did you hope to become Mistress of Bly? Because the truth is, you are in fact simply one mistress among thousands. Because it is thousands, you know, Miss Jessel. I have taken it upon myself to keep a running tabulation of his amorous adventures, entirely for my own amusement, of course. Your sisters in his affections include a cornucopia of variety artists, nude models, and the inhabitants of some of the finest Parisian brothels, as well as the wives and daughters of many of his closest friends, including, in one particularly memorable instance, a mother and her twin daughters. But you know all about that, don't you, Miss Jessel? You were, after all, the intimate friend of his dead sister-in-law, weren't you?

MISS JESSEL. Get away from me.

QUINT. Get away from you? You want me to get away from you? Well, I must confess, I'm confused, Miss Jessel. I'm having a bit of trouble following the trail of stale bread crumbs through your own personal emotional house of mirrors. First I was a horrible, horrible man. Then, for a time, I was, praise be to Her who dwells on high, actually considered to be a personage not entirely unworthy of your favors. Then the Master returns – just passing by in the rain, after a bit of card playing and carousing with the Devil and the Archbishop of Canterbury – that great, handsome, charming, amoral, cretinous, blathering satyr returns to the manor in his habitual state of elegant drunken rut, and suddenly I am invisible, fit only to shine shoes and fetch another bottle of cobwebbed port from the wine cellar. And yet now, abandoned once again by her beloved, the forlorn mistress and part time governess still considers herself too good to speak to Peter Quint, who is not a gentleman? What did you expect? What the hell did you expect, you magnificently stupid little trollop? Are you so monumentally blockheaded and utterly without self respect that you are able to convince yourself each time he appears that somehow this is the occasion upon which you will finally persuade him to beg on hands and knees and barking like a dog for your lily white hand in holy matrimony?

MISS JESSEL. Get away from me or I swear I will throw myself down from this tower. I will throw myself down from this place.

QUINT. Well, what a calamity that would be. We certainly don't want that, do we, Miss Jessel? If you were to smash your head into a pudding by leaping from the battlements of the tower, it would be a great inconvenience to the Master, now, wouldn't it? Why, he'd have to go to all the trouble of engaging a new governess, wouldn't he? Yes, that would serve him right. That would show him. He might frown for a full three minutes, learning of your unfortunate death. Not to mention the inconsolable grief of the children, who would have a holiday from their grotesquely distorted history lessons, and of Mrs Grose, who would have the unpleasant task of going out with a bucket of soapy water to scrape up your brains off the cobblestones.

MISS JESSEL. Have you no compassion at all?

QUINT. Compassion? You want me to have compassion? I who am not a gentleman? I who am but a gentleman's valet? The alleged Caretaker of Bly, who cannot take care of himself, let alone the poor wretched slut the Master has installed here to keep his brother's children from annoying him too much, somebody he can fornicate with on his rare visits to the family estates? You want my compassion, do you?

MISS JESSEL. I am leaving this place.

QUINT. You can't leave this place. You will never leave this place.

MISS JESSEL. If I stay here, I'll go mad.

(She starts to go.)

QUINT. *(Stopping her.)* But I am the Caretaker of Bly and I absoutely forbid it. Do you hear me? I forbid it. You must stay here and take your medicine like the rest of us.

MISS JESSEL. Let go of me. Let go.

QUINT. But Miss Jessel, if you should go away, what will become of the children? Would you leave them in the hands of a person who is not a gentleman?

MISS JESSEL. The children will survive.

QUINT. They've been abandoned by their poor dead parents, abandoned by their lecherous uncle, and now to be abandoned yet again by their beloved governess, a person they consider to be a veritable goddess – do you really think they can bear this? Miss Jessel, I must tell you, I simply can't be responsible for what might happen to the children if you go.

MISS JESSEL. What do you mean?

QUINT. I don't know if they could live through it.

MISS JESSEL. Is that a threat? Is that some sort of threat?

QUINT. A threat? Would I threaten a great lady like yourself? A gentleman might make threats, of course, but, as I think we have already established, I am not a gentleman.

MISS JESSEL. Peter, I know you would never harm those children. I have seen you with those children. You are gentle and patient and loving and wise with those children, and you make them laugh, and you care for them. You care for those children. You would never hurt them.

QUINT. Well, of course I would never hurt them. Not on purpose, at any rate. But any number of unfortunate things could happen to them when you're gone. They might fall out of the boat and drown in the lake. They might wander up to these battlements and plummet off the tower. They might tumble head first down the staircase. Or they might just stop breathing one night, in their sleep. That is, after all, the single most terrifying thing about children, isn't it, Miss Jessel? That anything could happen to them. Absolutely anything.

MISS JESSEL. Don't you see that I can't stay here? I must get out of this place. I must get out.

QUINT. I have been attempting to understand women, you know, Miss Jessel. I have been making a serious effort to comprehend the inner workings of what, for want of a better term, I like to think of as the female mind, and I am sorry to report that I am utterly defeated by this task. First they hate you, and then they love you, and they urge you to open up to them, to reveal to

them your innermost fears and secrets, and then, when
you do, when they are confident they have your complete and absolute trust and devotion, then they knife
you in the guts, and spit on your steaming intestines,
which they have carefully spilled out and arranged all
over the rose pattern carpet in the parlor, and then
they allow the most vile and despicable vermin in the
observable universe to violate them like the copulation of hyenas, and they do it right before your eyes, to
maximize your suffering, and then they accuse you of
being a monster, you of having no compassion. Where
the hell was your compassion when you allowed that
great miserable sadistic upperclass baboon to climb on
top of you again like a stallion mounting his favorite
donkey?

MISS JESSEL. If you had said one word to stop me, just one
word, I would not have done it. I swear I would not
have. Just one word from you.

QUINT. One word? One word? It was my job to say one
word to stop you? Please do not allow the Master to
thrust himself violently into your private parts? This is
how it becomes my fault? And what word would that
be, Miss Jessel? What word, exactly, what magic word
did you wish to hear?

MISS JESSEL. You are such a hypocrite. You are as much
under his spell as I am. Why did you let him go up
those stairs? Why did you not stop him? Why did you
not beat his brains out on the staircase, if you love me
so? Because you don't love me. You simply want me
because he has had me. You want what he has. You
want to possess all that he possesses. You want to be
him. Well, you can't have it, Peter. You can't be him
because you are not a gentleman, and you will never,
ever be a gentleman. You will forever be what you are,
which is a paid flunky who fetches the wine and shines
the shoes and listens to copulations with his ear to
the door. I'm am going now. Please have the carriage
brought round for me.

QUINT. *(Pulling her face to his and clutching her.)* If you go, I'll die. I will die. Do you understand me? I am not speaking metaphorically here, and I am not exaggerating. If you leave, I will die.

MISS JESSEL. You will not die.

QUINT. I will die. I will die. I will die.

MISS JESSEL. Do you want to kill me? Is that what you want? Because if I stay here, I am the one who will die. If you want me dead, if you hate me so much, then why don't you just put your hands around my throat and strangle me? Go on. Strangle me now and be done with it. You want to. But even that won't satisfy you, will it, Peter? Because it was never me that mattered, it was him. It was always him.

(Pause.)

QUINT. When I am dead, I will come back and haunt you.

MISS JESSEL. I am already haunted. I am haunted by the person in the mirror.

QUINT. I can't be without you. I can't. I can't.

MISS JESSEL. She is watching us now. I think she is always watching us. I have seen her watching from the mirror. I have seen her looking in the window, and across the lake. What if the children should see her? What if the children should see? What will she do to the children when you and I are gone? Peter, I think we have corrupted the children.

QUINT. No we haven't.

MISS JESSEL. I think we have. Oh, God, I think we have.

QUINT. No.

(He pulls her gently into his arms and holds her.)

MISS JESSEL. We have corrupted the children.

QUINT. We have not corrupted the children. The children have corrupted us. And when we are dead, we shall come back to haunt them, you and I. You and I. Together. Always together. Always.

(He holds her. The light fades on them and goes out.)

13

(Sound of a ticking clock. Lights up on a small writing desk. Morning at Bly. There is a sealed envelope on the desk. QUINT *moves into the light, sees the envelope, picks it up, turns it over, opens it with a letter opener. As he reads silently, lights up on* MISS JESSEL, *sitting on a bench in the park, speaking her letter.)*

MISS JESSEL. I've gone away. I know I swore to you last night that I would not, but when you were asleep I was awakened by the owls and I got up and looked into the mirror and saw her looking at me, looking, always looking. I simply cannot bear this any more. I've sent him a note to tell him. I could not bear to say goodbye to the children. You must tell them something. I don't know what. Tell them that I am ill. That must certainly be true. Tell them anything you like. It was only torture, being there. Please do not be angry with me. It is a kind of madness in my head. I have left not because I don't care for you. It's something else. It's the perverse recurring nightmare agony of it. I can't bear it. I hope you will not hate me. I think it's better if you and I do not communicate further. It is to spare your suffering as much as mine. Please do not think ill of me. The house is full of ghosts. I cannot look in the mirror. I know this will hurt you. It is a kind of madness.

(The light fades on her. She will remain on the bench through the next scene. QUINT *folds the letter, his face expressionless, puts it back in the envelope, puts the envelope in his pocket, sits down at the desk, picks up the letter opener, looks at his hands. The light fades on him. Sound of the ticking clock.)*

14

(Night. Moonlight. **QUINT** *on an icy road.)*

QUINT. The Caretaker of Bly stumbles along an icy road on a winter's night, and time is like a dream. They were both here once, and then he went, and then she went, and then Quint was alone. The Caretaker of Bly was alone. I had made of her a receptacle of lurid things. Perhaps we shall now enumerate the torments of the damned. I would lie awake at night and listen to the rain and watch her sleep. I am the hideous author of our woe. Christmas Eve in an old house. A ghostly winter's tale. Gruesome, gruesome. Her face in the shade of the great beech trees on a summer afternoon. Up the crooked staircase to the top of the old square tower. The empty dining room, a temple of mahogany and brass. I am dressed in another man's clothes, like a scarecrow. You are like nobody. You are like nobody's portrait. Her breasts. Kissing her breasts. Her sadness. Unfathomable. Ripping at my guts. In the inner chamber of my dread. You are much too familiar with the children, she said. You are much too familiar with everybody. Was I too familiar with you, Miss Jessel? Nothing is familiar now, here in the dark penultimate strangeness of our fate. The Master is not particular about the company he keeps. You are clever, Peter Quint, he said. You are deep. The Master believes in me, said Peter Quint. He thinks the country air will be good for my health. He thinks –

(He listens.)

Is somebody there? Is somebody there behind me on the icy path? There in the darkness, one who is always with me, who walks beside me, just to my left? Before the dawn of a winter's morning. It is steep here. One fatal slip in the dark. I think I have taken the wrong path altogether. At the bottom of which lay the corpse. He had taken a wrong turn in the night. There had been rumored matters in his life, strange passages and perils, secret disorders, vices more than anyone suspected. She, on the other hand, was a small, flat piece of wood with a little hole to put your finger in. Black is for mourning, blood-red for the copulation of demons. I have lived with a kind of fury of intention. I walk in shabby mourning clothes. I am infamous. She is infamous. We shall be infamous together. Impudent. Assured. Spoiled. Depraved. Fornicating with the maids. Let me put my hand upon the spot which aches. Is somebody there?

(He listens.)

She is gone from the house forever. My beloved is gone from the house forever. But I shall haunt her reflection in the mirror. I shall strangle her reflection in the mirror, I who have copulated with the finest barmaids have this night been disgusted by the slightest thought of any contact whatsoever with a soul who is not her. All I can see is her face. Those who love are doomed to haunt each other. I am haunted by the future of the past. I can see her naked in my head. Her flesh is devoured by pigs and satyrs. The beloved is covered with mud and spit, semen and blood and excrement and tears. I am a scarecrow in a field. A long walk in the cold, and a wrong turn in the dark. Except what then becomes of the children? The solemn little boy and the perfectly exquisite little girl with her button eyes. They are monstrous puppet images of us. They have spied upon us. The rooks have seen us from the battlements. I am devoured by owls on Christmas Eve. I am cold. I am cold. There are gargoyles in my head, eating my brains. And if I should stumble and fall and tumble down a steep incline on this icy night, and break open my scarecrow's head, will the darkness bleed out? Is somebody there in the dark just behind me? Is somebody there?

(The light fades on him and goes out.)

15

*(Bird sounds. Lights up on the park bench. **MISS JESSEL** is still sitting there. The **MASTER** strolls by. He stops.)*

MASTER. Miss Jessel?

MISS JESSEL. I'm sorry, sir, but as I am an extremely respectable young woman, I never speak to strange men in the park.

MASTER. Strange men? I am not a strange man. Well, perhaps I am a strange man, but that is entirely beside the point. Or perhaps not entirely beside the point, but nearly so. Where on earth have you been?

MISS JESSEL. I left.

MASTER. Yes, I know you left. I got your cryptic and vaguely demented note. We were all very worried about you.

MISS JESSEL. Were you? How exciting.

MASTER. Why did you leave? What happened to you?

MISS JESSEL. What happened to me, what happened to me was – I was unexpectedly called away on urgent business. Very urgent business.

MASTER. What kind of urgent business?

MISS JESSEL. Private business. I have a private world, you know, separate from yours. People do.

MASTER. I know people do. I didn't know you did.

MISS JESSEL. Well, now you know.

(Pause.)

Are the children well?

MASTER. I suppose they are. I've sent Miles off to boarding school, and I suppose I shall hire another governess to stay with Flora. There's nobody there to look after her now but Mrs Grose.

MISS JESSEL. And Peter Quint, of course. There is always Peter Quint.

MASTER. Peter Quint?

MISS JESSEL. Yes. Peter Quint. Your old friend Peter Quint. He is there to look after the children. You remember Peter Quint. He makes the children laugh.

MASTER. You don't know about poor Quint, then?

MISS JESSEL. What about him? He hasn't gone away, has he?

MASTER. No, he hasn't gone away. Well, in a manner of speaking he has. Peter Quint is dead.

MISS JESSEL. Is he?

MASTER. He was coming home from a visit to the pub in the village, very late on a bitterly cold night – you know Quint, had to have his barmaids, no matter what the season or the weather – and he seems to have taken a wrong turn in the dark, slipped on a steep, icy path and tumbled headlong into a ditch. A gravedigger found him, going to work in the morning. There was a large, ugly gash at the back of his head. Must have struck something sharp on the way down. It was not long after you left, actually. Perhaps it was Christmas Eve. Shame, really. Except of course he was going to die anyway, wasn't he? He wasn't well, you know.

MISS JESSEL. No. I know. He wasn't well. And, after all, he was only a servant, wasn't he?

MASTER. Nevertheless.

(Pause.)

You look very pale and cold there. Why don't you let me take you home?

MISS JESSEL. No thank you. I think not.

MASTER. It's no trouble, really. I mean, after all, you and I are old friends, aren't we?

MISS JESSEL. I don't think I wish to be taken home just now, thank you.

MASTER. At least stop in at my lodgings for a bit and have some tea, or chocolate, or a glass of wine. Warm up by the fire. It's just down the block there. You can see the front door from this bench, in fact. Well, you know where it is. You've been there.

MISS JESSEL. Yes, I have.

MASTER. So. Are you coming?

MISS JESSEL. I don't believe I am coming, no.

MASTER. *(Reaching down for her arm.)* Come on. You don't look well.

MISS JESSEL. *(Pulling her arm away violently.)* Get your filthy hands off me.

MASTER. I am only trying to –

MISS JESSEL. If you touch me again, I'll scream. If you touch me, I'll scream.

(She is sobbing. He holds her very tenderly in his arms.)

MASTER. I'll take you home and sit you by the fire and warm you up, and you'll feel better. I promise, you'll feel better. Perhaps I have not been kind. Perhaps I have not been kind.

(He holds her. The light fades on them and goes out.)

16

(Sound of a ticking clock. Lights up on **QUINT***, sitting in the Master's chair, before the embers of a fire at Bly, night.)*

QUINT. Embers. The ghost of Peter Quint looks into the embers of the fire on a winter's night, reflecting upon the geography of his own particular Hell. What is the true geography of Hell, he asks himself? Only this, he replies. Only this: that when one asks the question, one hears one's self reply. Only this.

(From the upstage darkness, **MISS JESSEL** *appears, looking at him. He does not see her yet.)*

To imagine where she is. To imagine what she is doing. To try not to imagine what she is doing. In death, all times and places coexist simultaneously, as in the pages of a book, as in the theatre, and thus, as in a theatre, all suffering is eternal and unredeemed, as in the pages of a book, and therefore –

(Pause. He sits staring into the fire.)

MISS JESSEL. I didn't know the dead sat by the fire.

(He looks up, but does not turn around. Pause.)

QUINT. Oh, yes. The dead often sit by the fire and burn regrets. What are you doing here?

MISS JESSEL. I've come back.

QUINT. You've come back?

MISS JESSEL. Yes. I've come back.

QUINT. *(Getting up and facing her.)* You wait until I'm dead and then you come back? Well, I'm afraid your presence here is no longer required, Miss Jessel. For you see, there is a new governess at Bly now, and we have no more need of you here, so why don't you just go away and leave us in peace?

MISS JESSEL. I don't think I can go away.

QUINT. Miss Jessel, I am dead. You are having a conversation

with a dead man. Are you not even the least bit dis-
turbed by this? And if you are not, shouldn't you be?
You believe that I am dead, don't you?

MISS JESSEL. Yes. I do.

QUINT. Well, I should think that might be sufficient to dis-
courage any decent person from attempting to engage
me in casual conversation, unless of course they have
the good fortune to be dead as well.

(He looks at her.)

Are you? My God, I believe you are.

MISS JESSEL. Yes, I think I must be. I think I must be dead
as well.

QUINT. And you've come back to haunt me? You've come
back to haunt me when I'm dead? Are you certain
you've entirely grasped the concept of what a ghost is,
Miss Jessel?

MISS JESSEL. Not you. I have not come back to haunt you,
Mr Quint. It's the children. I've come back to haunt
the children. Or perhaps it is not the children, exactly.
Perhaps it is the girl in the mirror. Perhaps it's her I've
come to haunt. She was always looking at me from
the mirror when I was alive, waiting there inside the
mirror to take my life from me, my job, my house,
my children, my lover, my soul. Perhaps we have now
simply exchanged places. Perhaps it is now my job to
drive her mad. I think that love is a kind of mutual
haunting. I have dreamed of this place every night,
you know. I mean of the children, and of the empty
halls and stairways of this place.

QUINT. But not of me.

MISS JESSEL. No. Not of you. Never of you.

QUINT. Are you quite certain of that?

MISS JESSEL. I have dreamed of the children sleeping
restlessly in their beds. I have not dreamed of you.
Although I have dreamed of somebody haunting
them. I have seen a face looking in the window at them

which was not entirely unlike your face. And I know she has seen my face when she looks in the mirror. The new governess, I mean. His latest conquest. The horrible, horrible, mad girl in the mirror. I've come back for the children, you see. Not for you. Not at all for you. I haven't come back for you.

QUINT. I think you have.

MISS JESSEL. Don't touch me. There is no touching in Hell.

QUINT. I think there is much copulation in Hell.

MISS JESSEL. Perhaps there is copulation in Hell, but there is no touching.

(Pause.)

QUINT. You are perfect in the firelight.

MISS JESSEL. You must not look at me that way.

QUINT. I was remembering touching you. Hell is the memory of touch. I think that you and I –

MISS JESSEL. I went to him.

QUINT. You went to him?

MISS JESSEL. Yes. When I was still alive, I mean. When I left you, I went to him. I sat on a bench in the cold for days in Regent's Park, just down the block from where he lives, and I waited for him to come by. I knew he would come, sooner or later. I know his habits, you see. I have studied his habits. I have memorized his habits.

QUINT. And did he come?

MISS JESSEL. Of course he came. He came upon me one day. And he was very sympathetic. And he took me back to his home. He was so tender and concerned for me. And he sat me in front of the fire. It was like a dream come true. And he gave me wine and took off my shoes and he rubbed my hands and feet. And he held me in his arms so tenderly, and comforted me, and kissed me. He was very gentle. I have never known him to be so gentle. It was wonderful. It was the most wonderful thing. It was almost as if he were my servant. And then he made love to me, there before the fire. And I cried and cried and cried, and he made love to me, and he made love to me.

(Pause. **QUINT** *sits down on the end of the love seat and rests his head in his hands.)*

Do you know why I cried, Peter Quint? Do you know why I cried? I cried because all I could see was your face. All the time that he was making love to me, all night, all I could see was your face. Oh, how I hate you. Do you know how much I hate you? Have you the slightest comprehension of how desperately I hate you?

(Pause.)

And then, when he was asleep, I put on my clothes and crept down the staircase and out of the house and walked to the river in the cold. The water is very cold, this time of year.

(Pause.)

What shall we do with the children, when we have got them?

QUINT. The children?

MISS JESSEL. Yes. We have both come here for the children, have we not? Not for each other. It's only for the children. We have come to claim our children. We are here not for each other, but for the children. What shall we do with the children, when we have got them?

QUINT. Teach them to love, like us.

(Pause.)

MISS JESSEL. Oh, what a horrible thing. What a horrible thing.

(She sits on the love seat, one hand resting on the space between them. **QUINT** *looks at her hand, then puts his hand on hers. Sound of the ticking clock. The light fades on them and goes out.)*

NOTEBOOK: QUINT AND MISS JESSEL AT BLY

Between September and December of the year 1897, having just signed a twenty-one year lease to Lamb House, his new home away from London, in Rye, on the Sussex coast, Henry James dictated at white heat the tale called "The Turn of the Screw," the idea for which had been fermenting in his brain since the Archbishop of Canterbury had related to him over dinner a fragmentary anecdote about the haunting of two children. Exactly one hundred years later, having just written, at white heat, two dark Christmas monologues, and still half drunk with an odd and ghostly Christmas mood, I found my mind suddenly filled with the image of Bly, the rook-haunted old country house in Essex, and of Quint and Miss Jessel, the ghosts who haunt it in James' story. I got my old green copy of "The Turn of the Screw" down off the shelf and read it again with a growing sense of wonder and of certainty.

In fact, I had begun the play a few weeks before the dark Christmas monologues, after reading a passionate and hopeless letter from Yeats to Maud Gonne, and it was to be about two other people entirely. But the lovers, once they'd begun clawing their way into the front chambers of my head, turned out to be Quint and Miss Jessel, could be nobody else, and the third part of the visible puzzle, I knew somehow with equal certainty, must be the charming but unreliable Master of Bly. The children must be imagined in the darkness. The other governess, the great and enigmatic heroine of James' story, must be herself a kind of ghost, a reflection in the mirror. For if the dead haunt the living, it seemed clear to me that in the world of this play the living must also haunt the dead. The madness of Miss Jessel is a mirror of the madness of her successor, who of course is not mad at all if the ghosts of Quint and Miss Jessel are real. But in the worlds I seem to be compelled to create to be enacted upon stages, there is forever a kind of ambiguity about the relative degrees of reality possessed by the characters, the players, the audience, and the author himself. My world is real enough to me because there is suffering in it. But it is also, at the same time, the reflection of an illusion. I see by reflected light, but so did James. What the Archbishop of Canterbury saw, I don't know.

There is a great joy in becoming lost in a created world, like the joy of dreaming a perfectly crafted dream. I have had dreams of such finely detailed wonderment that each brick in the brick wall of an old building was vivid and clear to me as I walked on a rainy day in my dream in a place I had not seen in many years. The closer to death, the more intense the memory. To sleep is to practice dying, and to die is to remember our death. It is the door to the imaginary place we were before we came onstage and took on the role that bears our name. When the door closes, there is silence in the empty theatre. James loved and hated the theatre, it seemed to him an impossibly vulgar and yet infinitely compelling phenomenon. He longed for the company and community of it even as he was horrified at its cruelty and venality. He wanted desperately the praise of an audience which simply didn't care to see his work. Defeated by the painted and treacherous world of the stage, he retreated to Rye and wrote tremendous things. It is often the case that out of despair and humiliation comes a precious and unexpected gift to be fashioned and given. Quint and Miss Jessel, reflected in the dark mirror of art, are ghosts more real than I am.

Some plays take a long time to develop after one begins writing them, and are put aside and taken up again many times over the course of weeks, months, years, even decades before they are finished. Other times, the play just comes flooding out from some dark place in one's soul and one is pulled along in the torrent, grateful, a bit alarmed, but in a state of weird creative ecstasy which must be akin to what the mystic feels who has fallen into a trance. I don't know why this play came on me so violently all of a sudden one day in September exactly one hundred years after Mr James wrote his extraordinary and enigmatic tale, or why I could think of nothing else until it was done. It doesn't always happen this way, but when it does, one must get the thing down before the voice grows silent. That is all I know, or all I need to know about it. We work in the dark, James said, we do what we can – we give what we have. Our doubt is our passion and our passion is our task. The rest is the madness of art.

ABOUT THE AUTHOR

Among the most frequently published and widely produced playwrights in the world, DON NIGRO has continued to build a deeply inter-related but remarkably diverse body of dramatic literature over the years, work that is often mysterious and unclassifiable, employing a wide variety of dramatic conventions and styles of presentation. He has written monologues and epics, spare realistic dramas and surreal homicidal puppet farces, plays with music and verse plays. He continues to build the long cycle of Pendragon County plays, which traces the history of America through the lives of several related east Ohio families from the eighteenth century to the present, and features many characters whose lives are followed from youth through middle-age to old age in a number of plays designed to be presented in a variety of different combinations. Nigro has twice been a finalist for the National Repertory Theatre Foundation's National Play Award, and has won a Playwriting Fellowship Grant from the National Endowment for the Arts and grants from the Ohio Arts Council and the Mary Roberts Rinehart Foundation. He has twice been James Thurber Writer in Residence at the Thurber House in Columbus.

His work has been translated into French, Italian, Spanish, German, Polish, Greek, Russian and Chinese. John Clancy's production of Nigro's *Cincinnati*, featuring Nancy Walsh, won Fringe First and Spirit of the Fringe awards at the Edinburgh Fringe Festival, Best of Fringe at the Adelaide Fringe Festival, and has toured Britain. *Seascape With Sharks And Dancer* has been in the repertory of Teatr Syrena in Warsaw, and *Lucia Mad* was produced at Teatr Julius Slowakie in Krakow and the Teatro del Fantasma has presented a Spanish translation of *The Girlhood of Shakespeare's Heroines* in Mexico City. *Widdershins* was produced as part of the first International Mystery Festival. Nigro's plays have also been produced in Singapore, Hong Kong and Beijing, and toured India. SpielArt, based in Munich, has translated and toured two productions of his plays in Germany.

His work is produced every year in a variety of New York theatres, and has been done at the Oregon Shakespeare Festival, the McCarter Theatre, Actors Theatre of Louisville, Capital Repertory Company, the Hypothetical Theatre, the Berkeley Stage Company, Manhattan Class Company, the People's Light and Theatre Company, Theatre X, Shadowbox Cabaret, the Hudson Guild Theatre, the WPA Theatre, and many others, in every state.

Born in 1949 in Canton, Ohio, Nigro grew up in Ohio and Arizona. He has a BA in English from The Ohio State University and an MFA in Dramatic Arts from the Playwrights Workshop at the University of Iowa. Nigro has taught courses in Comparative Literature, Dramatic Literature and playwriting at Ohio State, Iowa, Kent State, Indiana State, and the University of Massachusetts at Amherst. *Grotesque Lovesongs* was translated and produced on Polish television, and the film *The Manor*, with Peter O'Toole, is based on his play *Ravenscroft*. Forty-eight volumes of his plays have been published by Samuel French. The Don Nigro Collection at the Jerome Lawrence and Robert E. Lee Theatre Research Institute at the Ohio State University contains a growing repository for his manuscripts and other materials.

Also by
Don Nigro...

Joan of Arc in the Autumn
The King of the Cats
Laestrygonians
The Last of the Dutch Hotel
The Lost Girl
Loves Labours Wonne
Lucia Mad
Lucy and the Mystery of the
  Vine Encrusted Mansion
Lurker
MacNaughton's Dowry
Madeline Nude in the
  Rain Perhaps
Madrigals
Major Weir
The Malefactor's
  Bloody Register
Mariner
Mink Ties
Monkey Soup
Mooncalf
Mulberry Street
My Sweetheart's The
  Man in the Moon
Narragansett
Necropolis
Netherlands
Nightmare with Clocks
November
Paganini
Palestrina
Panther
Pendragon
Pendragon Plays
Picasso
Ragnarok

Rat Wives
Ravenscroft
The Reeves Tale
Rhiannon
Ringrose the Pirate
Robin Hood
The Rooky Wood
Scarecrow
Seance
Seascape with Sharks
  and Dancer
The Sin-Eater
Something in the Basement
Sorceress
Specter
Squirrels (Nigro)
Sudden Acceleration
Sycorax
Tainted Justice
The Tale of the Johnson Boys
Tales from the Red Rose Inn
Things That Go Bump
  in the Night
The Transylvanian Clockworks
Tristan
Uncle Clete's Toad
Warburton's Cook
The Weird Sisters
Widdershins
Wild Turkeys
Winchelsea Dround
Within the Ghostly
Mansion's Labyrinth
Wolfsbane
The Wonders of the
  Invisible World Revealed
The Woodman and the Goblins

Please visit our website **samuelfrench.com** for complete
descriptions and licensing information

OTHER TITLES AVAILABLE FROM SAMUEL FRENCH

WIDDERSHINS

Don Nigro

4m, 6f / Interior

Inspector Ruffing, the troubled hero of Nigro's *Ravenscroft, Demonology, Creatures Lurking In The Churchyard, The Rooky Wood* and *Mephisto* returns in this baffling mystery that was an audience favorite at the First International Mystery Festival in 2007. In a peaceful house near the Welsh border, an entire family has vanished suddenly without a trace one evening with supper on the table and no apparent violence. Ruffing's attempt to understand what's happened to a couple and their two daughters leads him deep into his own dark soul. The only clue is a piece of paper left on a desk with the word 'Widdershins' written on it. Beautiful women, dark secrets, the Impressionists and the Druids all figure in this unusual and thought provoking play.

OTHER TITLES AVAILABLE FROM SAMUEL FRENCH

MY SWEETHEART'S THE MAN IN THE MOON

Don Nigro

Dramatic Comedy / 2m, 3f / Unit set.

In the first years of the twentieth century, Evelyn Nesbit, the beautiful, teen-age pin up and chorus girl, was the entrancing center of an explosive and deadly love triangle involving Stanford White, her married lover and the architect of many of the most famous buildings in New York, who liked to push her naked on a red velvet swing, and Harry K. Thaw, the wealthy, manic and demented roller-skating Pittsburgh playboy who married her, beat her with a horse whip, and eventually shot White through the eye socket during a musical performance at the rooftop theatre at White's Madison Square Garden. This wickedly funny play chronicles the grotesque events leading up to and after this notorious murder and Evelyn's wild, strange journey through her American tabloid nightmare as she is hounded by carnivorous reporters, threatened, used, betrayed, bribed, stalked and nearly destroyed by the rich, the corrupt, the violent and the insane. Part of Nigro's ongoing dramatic saga of America in the 20th century that continues with Jules Verne Eats a Rhinoceros, City of Dreadful Night and Traitors, Originally produced at the Open Stage Theatre in Pittsburgh and Off Broadway by the Hypothetical Theatre Company.

"Literate but quirky ... non-realistic theatricality ... smartly ironic ..."
– *Pittsburgh Post-Gazette*

"There was a bit of everything: wealth, fame, insanity, genius, and, in the middle of it all, a beautiful chorus girl ... The sensational story has been adapted for screen and stage ... but the latest play, Don Nigro's "*My Sweetheart's The Man In The Moon*," might be its most faithful version. It demonstrates admirable nuance and an impressive amount of research ..."
– *The New York Times*

"People who think Evelyn Nesbit is only a fictional character from *Ragtime* may find some surprises in Don Nigro's play, which chronicles the tawdry, twisted love triangle that "the girl in the red velvet swing" shared with master architect (and seducer) Stanford White and millionaire psychopath Harry K. Thaw."
– *Village Voice*